COOK-A-DOODLE-DOO!

Janet Stevens AND Susan Stevens Crummel

ILLUSTRATED BY JANET STEVENS

Voyager Books
Harcourt, Inc.

Orlando   Austin   New York   San Diego   Toronto   London

Text copyright © 1999 by Janet Stevens and Susan Stevens Crummel
Illustrations copyright © 1999 by Janet Stevens

www.HarcourtBooks.com

First Voyager Books edition 2005
Voyager Books is a trademark of Harcourt, Inc., registered in the
United States of America and/or other jurisdictions.

The Library of Congress has cataloged the hardcover edition as follows:
Stevens, Janet.
Cook-a-doodle-doo!/written by Janet Stevens and
Susan Stevens Crummel; illustrated by Janet Stevens.
p. cm.
Summary: With the questionable help of his friends, Big Brown
Rooster manages to bake a strawberry shortcake which would
have pleased his great-grandmother, Little Red Hen.
[1. Cake—Fiction. 2. Baking—Fiction. 3. Roosters—Fiction.
4. Animals—Fiction.]
I. Crummel, Susan Stevens. II. Title.
PZ7.S8447Co 1999
[E]—dc21 98-8853
ISBN 0-15-201924-3
ISBN 0-15-205658-0 pb

H G F E D C

The illustrations in this book were done in watercolor, colored pencil,
gesso, and photographic and digital elements on paper made by hand by
Ray Tomasso, Denver, Colorado.
The display type was set in Fontesque and Colwell.
The text type was set in Goudy Catalogue.
Color separations by Bright Arts Ltd,, Hong Kong
Manufactured by South China Printing Company, Ltd., China
Production supervision by Ginger Boyer
Designed by Lydia D'moch

Special thanks to Sherwood, Tom, and Ted—
and thanks to all the kids, teachers, and parents
who helped me name this book.

—J. S.

Special thanks to Richard and Priscilla.

—S. S. C.

To the most wonderful, magnificent cooks in the whole wide world—
our mother, Frances, and our grandmother, Esther

—J. S. AND S. S. C.

Peck. Peck. Peck.

"Always chicken feed! Day after day—year after year—I'm sick of it!" squawked Big Brown Rooster. "Can we get something new to eat around here? Please? Nobody's listening. What's a hungry rooster to do?"

"There's no hope. Wait a minute . . ." Rooster remembered a story his mama used to tell, a story handed down from chicken to chicken. The story of his famous great-grandmother, the Little Red Hen.

Rooster rushed into the chicken coop. "It has to be here," he said. He looked high and low, and there it was at last, hidden under a nest—her cookbook. *The Joy of Cooking Alone* by L. R. Hen.

Rooster carefully turned the pages. "So many recipes—and I thought she just baked bread! Look at the strawberry shortcake!"

Little Red Hen's Magnificent Strawberry Shortcake

"That's it! I'll make the most wonderful, magnificent strawberry shortcake in the whole wide world. No more chicken feed for me!"

"Yes sirree—just like Great-Granny, I'll be a cook!
COOK-A-DOODLE-DO-O-O!" crowed Rooster
as he pranced toward the big farmhouse.

"Cook-a-doodle-doo?" said Dog.

"Have you lost your marbles, Rooster?" asked Cat.

"You've never cooked anything before!" said Goose.

"That doesn't matter," replied Rooster. "Cooking is in my blood—it's a family tradition. Now, who will help me?"

"Not I," said Dog.

"Not I," said Cat.

"Not I," said Goose.

And away they went.

Rooster pushed open the kitchen door. "It looks like I'm on my own . . . just like Great-Granny." He sighed and put on his apron.

"We'll help you."

Rooster turned, and there stood Turtle, Iguana, and Potbellied Pig.

"Do you three know anything about cooking?" Rooster asked.

"I can read recipes!"
said Turtle.
   "I can get stuff!"
said Iguana.
   "I can taste!" said Pig.
"I'm an expert at tasting."

"Then we're a team," declared Rooster.
"Let's get ready and start cooking!"

Turtle read the cookbook.
"Heat oven to 450 degrees."

"I can do that!" said Iguana.
"Look, I'll turn the knob. 150,
250, 350, 450. Hey, cooking
is easy!"

A cookbook gives directions for making many different things to eat. Each type of food has its own recipe—a list of everything that goes into it and step-by-step directions on how to make it.

One of the oven knobs controls the temperature of the oven. The higher the number on the knob, the hotter the oven. Temperature is measured in degrees Fahrenheit (°F) or degrees Celsius (°C). On a very hot day the temperature outside can be over 100°F (38°C). Can you imagine what 450°F (232°C) feels like?

Ingredients are the different things that go into a recipe. Each ingredient may not taste good by itself, but if you put them all together in the right way, the result tastes delicious.

Make sure you use a big bowl that will hold all of the ingredients. It's best to set out everything before you start cooking, so you don't have to go looking for your ingredients one-by-one like Iguana!

Rooster put a big bowl on the table. "What's our first ingredient?" he asked.

"The recipe says we need flour," said Turtle.

"I can do that!" said Iguana. He dashed outside and picked a petunia. "How's this flower?"

Flour is made from wheat grains that are finely ground. Long ago, the grinding was done by hand; now it is done by machines. Rooster's Great-Granny had to grind the grain into flour by hand, but you and Rooster can buy flour at the grocery store.

You will find many different kinds of flour at the store—including all-purpose flour, whole-wheat flour, cake flour, and high-altitude flour. Rooster's recipe calls for all-purpose flour.

"No, no, no," said Rooster. "Not *that* kind of flower. We need flour for *cooking*. You know, the fluffy white stuff that's made from wheat."

"Can I taste the flour?" asked Pig.

"Not yet, Pig," said Turtle. "The recipe says to sift it first."

"What does *sift* mean?" asked Iguana.

"Hmmm," said Turtle. "I think *sift* means 'to search through' . . ."

"You mean like when I sift through the garbage looking for lunch?" asked Pig.

"I can do that!" said Iguana. And he dived into the flour, throwing it everywhere!

Sifting adds air to the flour so it can be measured accurately. Some sifters have cranks, some have spring-action handles, and some are battery powered.

Make sure you put waxed paper on the counter before you start sifting. It will make cleanup a lot easier!

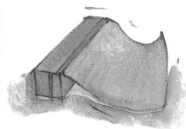

"No, no, no," said Rooster. "Don't sift the flour like that. Put it through this sifter." Rooster turned the crank and sifted the flour into a big pile. "Can I taste the pile?" asked Pig.

"Not yet, Pig," said Turtle. "Now we measure the flour."

"I can do that!" said Iguana. He grabbed a ruler. "The flour is four inches tall."

Measuring cups for dry ingredients are made of metal or plastic and usually come in sets of four—1 cup, 1/2 cup, 1/3 cup, and 1/4 cup. Pick the measuring cup that holds the amount you need, then dip it into the dry ingredient, getting a heaping amount. Level it off with the straight edge of a knife and let the extra fall back into the container  (although Pig would be very happy if just a little fell on the floor!).

Dry ingredients can be measured in cups or grams.

1 cup = 227 grams
2 cups = 454 grams

"No, no, no," said Rooster. "We don't want to know how *tall* it is. We want to know how *much* there is. We measure the flour with this metal measuring cup."

"We need two cups," added Turtle. "So fill it twice."

Rooster dumped the two cups of flour into the bowl.

"Can I taste it *now*?" asked Pig.

"Not yet, Pig," said Turtle. "Next we add two tablespoons of sugar, one tablespoon of baking powder, and one-half teaspoon of salt."

"I can do that!" said Iguana. He looked under the table. "But where are the tablespoons?" He looked in the teapot. "No teaspoons in here!"

Some ingredients are included for flavor, but not baking powder. Even Pig thinks it tastes terrible! When baking powder is added to the shortcake, bubbles of gas form and get bigger while the cake bakes, which makes it rise.

Dry ingredients are all sifted together so they will be evenly mixed.

Iguana wasn't far off when he looked for tablespoons under the table and teaspoons in the teapot. Tablespoons were named after the large spoons used at the table to serve soup, and teaspoons after the smaller spoons used to stir tea.

3 teaspoons = 1 tablespoon = 14 grams

"No, no, no," said Rooster. "Don't look in the teapot or under the table! These spoons are for measuring. Each holds a certain amount." Rooster measured the sugar, baking powder, and salt, poured them into the big bowl, then sifted all the dry ingredients together.

"Looks awfully white in there," said Pig. "I better taste it."

"Not yet, Pig," said Turtle. "Now we add butter. We need one stick."

"I can do that!" cried Iguana. He raced outside and broke off a branch. "How's this stick?"

Butter is made by churning cream, the fat in cow's milk. (This doesn't mean it comes from a fat cow!)

Margarine can be used instead of butter. Butter and margarine come in sticks and are easy to measure because their wrappers are marked in tablespoons.

1 stick butter = 1/2 cup = 8 tablespoons = 113 grams

"No, no, no," said Rooster. "Not *that* kind of stick. A stick of *butter*." Rooster unwrapped the butter and dropped it into the bowl.

"That butter is just sitting there like a log," said Pig. "Maybe I need to taste it."

"Not yet, Pig," said Turtle. "Next we cut in the butter."

"I can do that!" said Iguana. "Uh-oh. Scissors don't cut butter very well."

Butter and margarine are two types of solid shortening, or fat, used in cooking. The name "shortcake" doesn't mean the cake is short—it refers to the shortening in the recipe.

Cool butter is "cut in" to dry ingredients by using two table knives or a pastry blender. Cut the butter into tiny pieces.

"No, no, no," said Rooster. "Don't cut the butter with scissors. Use these two table knives, like this."

Rooster cut in the butter until the mixture was crumbly.

"Looks mighty dry in there," said Pig. "Perhaps I should taste it."

"Not yet, Pig," said Turtle.
"Now the recipe says to beat
one egg."

"I can do that!" cried Iguana.

Break an egg by hitting the shell gently on the edge of a countertop or bowl to make a small crack. Place both thumbs in the crack and pull the shell apart. Always crack an egg into a small bowl before you add it to the other ingredients in case the egg is bad or shell pieces fall in. Eggs add color and flavor and help hold the cake together.

 You can beat the eggs with a fork, a hand beater (like Rooster's), or an electric mixer. If you use an electric mixer, make sure to put the eggs in a big bowl and start off on a low speed. If you start with the mixer on high, you'll get egg on your face!

"No, no, no," said Rooster. "Don't beat an egg with a baseball bat! We use an eggbeater." Rooster carefully broke the egg into a dish, beat it with the eggbeater, and poured it into the big bowl.

"That looks tasty," said Pig. "Please let me taste it."

"Not yet, Pig," said Turtle. "Now add milk. We need two-thirds of a cup."

"I can do that!" said Iguana. "Here, hold that glass measuring cup and I'll saw off a third. We'll use the other two-thirds to measure the milk."

"Wait," said Pig. "Why don't we fill the measuring cup to the top and I'll drink down a third?"

Liquid measuring cups are made of glass or plastic. Each measuring cup has a spout for pouring and extra room below the rim so you don't have to fill it to the top and worry about spilling. Always put the cup on a flat surface and measure at eye level.

Grease the pan with a solid shortening so the cake will not stick.

Rooster is mixing the batter by hand, which means to stir with a spoon instead of a mixer. (How would Iguana mix by hand?)

"No, no, no," said Rooster. "The cup has marks on it— 1/3—2/3—1 cup. We'll fill it to the 2/3 mark." Rooster poured the milk into the bowl.

"It surely needs tasting now!" said Pig.

"Not yet, Pig," said Turtle. "Now we mix the dough and put it in a greased baking pan." Rooster stirred and spread as Turtle read, "Bake in the oven for fifteen to eighteen minutes."

"I can do that!" cried Iguana.

Make sure you stay nearby, so you can hear the timer when your cake is ready! Cooking times are given in hours, minutes, or seconds.

1 hour = 60 minutes

1 minute = 60 seconds

Wash the strawberries first and cut off their tops. Use a cutting board and cut each strawberry in half, then cut each half in half. (How many pieces do you have now?) Watch out for your fingers!

Whipping cream comes from cow's milk. It contains more butterfat than regular cream. Iguana might think you use a whip to whip the cream, but you could use an eggbeater or electric mixer.

Iguana shoved the pan into the oven. "Let's see, fifteen minutes equals nine hundred seconds. I'll count them. One, two, three, four—"

"No, no, no," said Rooster, and he set the timer so that Iguana would stop counting the seconds. Pig burned his tongue on the oven door trying to taste the shortcake. Turtle studied the cookbook to see what to do next.

"Let's cut up the strawberries and whip the cream," said Turtle.

And they cut and cut and whipped and whipped, until . . . *ding!*

When you take something out of a hot oven, make sure you use a pot holder or oven mitt.

A trick to tell if your shortcake is done: Stick a toothpick or knife in the center of the cake. If it comes out clean, without any cake sticking to it, the shortcake is ready.

Don't forget to turn off the oven when you're finished!

Rooster grabbed the oven mitt off Iguana's head and took the shortcake carefully out of the oven.

"Oh, it's beautiful, and it smells *sooo* good," said Pig. "I know I have to taste it now."

"Not yet, Pig," said Turtle. "We need to let it cool."

Soon the shortcake was ready to cut. Rooster sliced it in half.

They stacked one layer of cake, one layer of whipped cream, one layer of strawberries.

Then again—cake,   cream,   berries.

It looked just like the picture of the strawberry shortcake in the cookbook.
"This is the most wonderful, magnificent strawberry shortcake in the whole wide world," said Rooster. "If Great-Granny could see me now! Let's take it to the table."

"I can do that!" cried Iguana.

He yanked at the plate. The shortcake tilted . . . and slid . . .

splat!

Right on the floor.

Pig was ready. "Now it's my turn—to taste it!" In a split second the strawberry shortcake was gone. Every last crumb had disappeared into the potbelly of the pig.

"Our shortcake!" Iguana cried. "You ate it!"

"I thought it was my turn," replied Pig. "I'm the taster, remember? And it tasted great!"

"But it was our masterpiece," moaned Turtle.

"And a tasty one, too," said Pig. "Now we can make something else."

"Yeah . . ." Iguana glared. "How about a plump, juicy roast pig?"

Pig gasped. "Roast pig? How about iguana potpie—or—or—turtle soup!"

"No, no, no!" cried Rooster. "Listen to me! We made this shortcake as a team, and teams work together."

"But Pig ate it!" whined Turtle.

"Iguana dropped it," pouted Pig.

"Turtle should have caught it," grumbled Iguana.

"It doesn't matter," said Rooster. "The first shortcake was just for practice. It won't be as hard to make the second time!"

"Well," added Turtle, "we don't have to worry about messing up the kitchen. It's already a mess."

"So, who will help me make it again?" asked Rooster.

Pig, Turtle, and Iguana looked at each other.

"I will!" said Pig.

"I will!" said Turtle.

"I will!" said Iguana.

"Cook-a-doodle-dooooo!" crowed Rooster. "Let's get cooking again!"

Together they made the second most wonderful, magnificent strawberry shortcake in the whole wide world. And it was a lot easier than the first time!

The JOY of
Cooking Together
by B.B. Rooster
and Friends

Great-Granny's Magnificent Strawberry Shortcake

2 cups all-purpose flour, sifted
2 tablespoons sugar
1 tablespoon baking powder
½ teaspoon salt
½ cup butter
1 egg, beaten
⅔ cup milk
3 to 4 cups strawberries, washed and sliced
1 cup whipping cream, whipped

Preheat oven to 450° Fahrenheit. Sift flour, then sift together dry ingredients. Cut in butter until mixture resembles coarse crumbs. Add egg and milk, stirring by hand just enough to moisten. Spread dough in greased 8 x 1½-inch round pan, building up edges slightly. Bake for 15 to 18 minutes. Remove cake from pan; cool on rack 5 minutes. Split into two layers; lift top off carefully. Alternate layers of cake, whipped cream, and strawberries, ending with strawberries on top.